GRIZZLYSHARK

BY
RYAN OTTLEY
STORY, ART, & LETTERS

COLORS BY
IVAN PLASCENCIA

KELSEY SHANNON
CHAPTER 1 COVER COLORS
FCO PLASCENCIA
CHAPTERS 2 & 3 COVER COLORS

BOOK DESIGN BY
RUS WOOTON
LOGO DESIGN BY
COMICRAFT

GRIZZLYSHARK VOL. 1. FIRST PRINTING. SEPTEMBER 2016.
ISBN 978-1-63215-884-0

GRIZZLYSHARK
OTTLEY
+KELSEY

I GOTTA PEE.
WHAT ARE YOU A FLIPPIN' IDIOT? YA DON'T GO WANDERING IN THESE WOODS WITHOUT A GUN.
KRAK
THERE ARE SHARKS IN THESE WOODS!
OW GEEZ DAD. YER PARANOID AND CRAZY. BEARS ARE IN THESE WOODS, NOTHING ELSE!
THOSE TEETH BITES ON MY CATTLE ARE NOT FROM BEARS! I KNOW SHARK BITES WHEN I SEE 'EM!
YEAH WHATEVER
YEAH WELL, UNCLE CARL AND JONBOB ARE BRINGING A SPECIALIST IN, HE'LL SHOW YOU!
YOU BETTER TAKE CARE OF THAT WOUND, SHARKS CAN SMELL BLOOD FOR A HUNDRED MILES!

DAD YOU'RE SUCH AN IDIO... WTF ?!?
SON OF A..
MUNCH
DAMMIT DONNIE, MOVE ASIDE SO I CAN GET A CLEAR SHOT!
I'M TRYING TO!

BOOM
RAWR
DONNIE! YOU OKAY?
I'M DYING DADDY.
NOT ON MY WATCH YOU AINT. WE GOTTA CAUTERIZE THE WOUND!
ARRGH
TSSSS
IT HURTS REAL BAD!
STOP YOUR COMPLAINING. I JUST SAVED YOUR LIFE. SHOW SOME GRATITUDE.
HERE, TAKE A FEW ASPIRIN.
ASPIRIN

GULP
SON NO! THAT'S TOO MANY! WHAT DO YOU GOT A DEATH WISH?
DON'T WORRY DAD. I'M GONNA BE OK.
MY STOMACH IS OVER THERE.
HA HA!
WHA?
HA HA HA HA HA HA HA HA HA HA HA HA HA HA HA HA HA

ELSEWHERE...
GUNS N' SUCH
RASKIN BOBBINS
OK SO HERE'S THE DEAL, PETE GAVE ME 100 BUCKS FOR SUPPLIES AND AMMO. AS SOON AS WE KILL WHATEVER'S BEEN EATING PETE'S CATTLE HE'll PAY YOU YOUR FEE.
WELL I WANT ICE CREAM NOW.
YOU CAN TAKE IT FROM MY FEE LATER.
OH. OK HURRY AND GET YOUR ICE CREAM AND BRING ME BACK THE CHANGE, K?
WILL DO!
WHAT SHOULD I DO UNCLE CARL?
YOU JUST SIT THERE AND LOOK PRETTY JONBOB.
AHAH!!! UH-UH!

I'LL TAKE A LARGE CINNAMON BEAR JUBILEE!
YUM
SORRY THAT FLAVOR IS SEASONAL, WE'LL BE SERVING THAT STARTING TOMORROW.
NO NO NO
WHAT THE ?
YOU GOTTA TRY THIS CINNAMON BEAR JUBILEE, HOTTEST CINNAMON BEARS EVER!
IT'S LIKE ICE COLD AND RED HOT AT THE SAME TIME.
SO... WHERE'S MY CHANGE?
RIGHT HERE! THIS DRUM COST ME 99.50. JUST TAKE FROM MY FEE, NOT A PROBLEM.
BUT... UH...
HEY, I ASKED FOR A NORMAL SIZE! THIS FLAVOR IS SEASONAL. YA CAN'T WAIT ON THIS STUFF.
THE GUY SAID HE WAS ONLY ALLOWED TO SELL THE ENTIRE DRUM BEFORE THE ESTABLISHED DATE.
SO I SLAMMED MY MONEY DOWN CUZ I DON'T TAKE NO CRAP FROM NOBODY.
I SHOWED HIM!
AND HEY. IT'S NOT LIKE I WON'T SHARE.

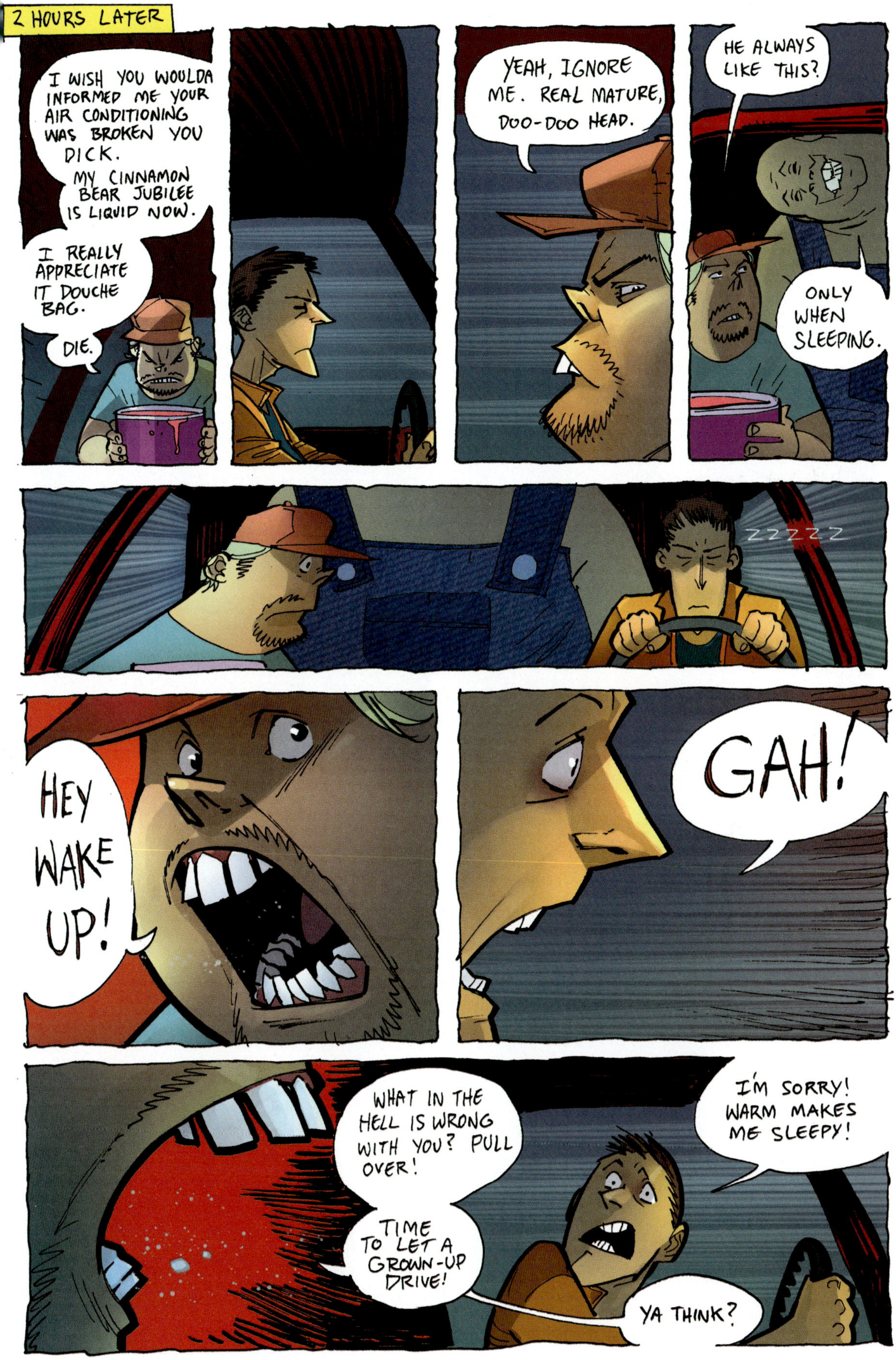
2 HOURS LATER
I WISH YOU WOULDA INFORMED ME YOUR AIR CONDITIONING WAS BROKEN YOU DICK.
MY CINNAMON BEAR JUBILEE IS LIQUID NOW.
I REALLY APPRECIATE IT DOUCHE BAG.
DIE.
YEAH, IGNORE ME. REAL MATURE, DOO-DOO HEAD.
HE ALWAYS LIKE THIS?
ONLY WHEN SLEEPING.
ZZZZZ
HEY WAKE UP!
GAH!
WHAT IN THE HELL IS WRONG WITH YOU? PULL OVER!
TIME TO LET A GROWN-UP DRIVE!
I'M SORRY! WARM MAKES ME SLEEPY!
YA THINK?

JUST WATCH THE ROAD WILL YA?
WHA?
THUMP
SKREEEEEEEEEEEEE
SLAM
NO!

I SAVED AMMO ON THIS ONE.
OH DEER!
THANKS FELLA'S!
OH DEER!
HEY, YOU FELLAS OK?
AAAAAAA
ARRGH
IT BURNS THE EYES!
OH THE GORE!!
ACK!

1 MILE AWAY...
DAD? I GOTTA PEE.
WHAT THE? HOW...
HAHA
HA HA HA HA HA HA HA HA HA HA HA

TRIP
AGH!
GAH!
KRAK
WHEW, I'M OK.
I'M NOT! LOOKIT THE BLOOOD!!
DONNIE, WE GOTTA GET MOVING, QUICK.
GRRRRR
CRAP, WE'RE TOO LATE! SHH, JUST STAY STILL. HE CAN'T SEE US IF WE STAY STILL.
DAD, I THINK THAT'S DINOSAURS YOU'RE THINKIN' ABOUT.
OH YEAH.
RUSTLE RUSTLE

RAWR
RUN!
HEY!

I HAVE NEVER BEEN SO STICKY IN ALL MY LIFE! AND THESE BUGS! MOSQUITO BITES ON TOP OF MOSQUITO BITES!
LISTEN CARL, I'M GONNA NEED FULL REIMBURSEMENTS FOR THIS CRAP. EVERYTHING THAT WAS DESTROYED, MY CLOTHES, MY DRUM OF ICE CREAM, MY HAT, MY PACK OF GUM. I DON'T KNOW HOW MANY HOURS OF THERAPY I NEED JUST FROM SEEING THAT POOR HUNTER DIE OF A HEART ATTACK, BUT IT WILL BE CONSIDERABLE.
UNCLE PETE IS THE BEST UNCLE I GOT SO TRUST ME GARY, HE'LL COMPENSATE YOU FULLY, NO DOUBT
HELP ME!
HE GOT DONNIE, WE GOTTA RUN!
OH! HEY PETE! SO FUNNY, WE WAS JUST TALKING ABOUT YOU! THIS IS "EXTERMINATOR GARY, KILLER OF ALL THINGS SCARY." LIKE WE SAW ON T.V.!
NICE TO MEET YOU PETE. NOW ABOUT MY FEE I NEED TRIPLED.
WHATEVER YOU WANT! JUST KILL IT!!!
KILL IT NOW!

AAAAAA!
LICK
BLEH.
WTF OMG
HE LEFT!! HOW'D YOU DO THAT?!?
UH... UM... WELL...
OH.
WELL WHY WOULD WE GO INTO THE WOODS WITHOUT WEARING MY CINNAMON BEAR JUBILEE SHARK REPELLANT BODY SPREAD?
PATENT PENDING.
AMAZING!
UNCLE PETE, WE REALLY SHOULD BE GOING. WHERE'S THAT CABIN OF YOURS?
SHOULD BE CLOSE. ONCE WE GET TO THE TOP OF THIS RIDGE I'LL KNOW WHERE WE ARE.
THANK GOODNESS WE GOT GARY HERE. I FEEL MUCH SAFER!
SO WHERE DO YOU THINK THAT SHARK RAN OFF TO?
HE'S PROBABLY OFF SEARCHING FOR PREY THAT IS A BIT MORE APPETIZING.
YEAH. THAT OR LOOKING FOR TASTIER FOOD.

AH POOP, I GOT A PAPERCUT ON THESE DARN SHARP ROCKS.

MUNCH

DAMMIT DARLING! WILL YOU STOP ASKING ME QUESTIONS WHILE I'M EATING?! I JUST BIT MY TONGUE BECAUSE OF YOU!
SORRY DEAR.

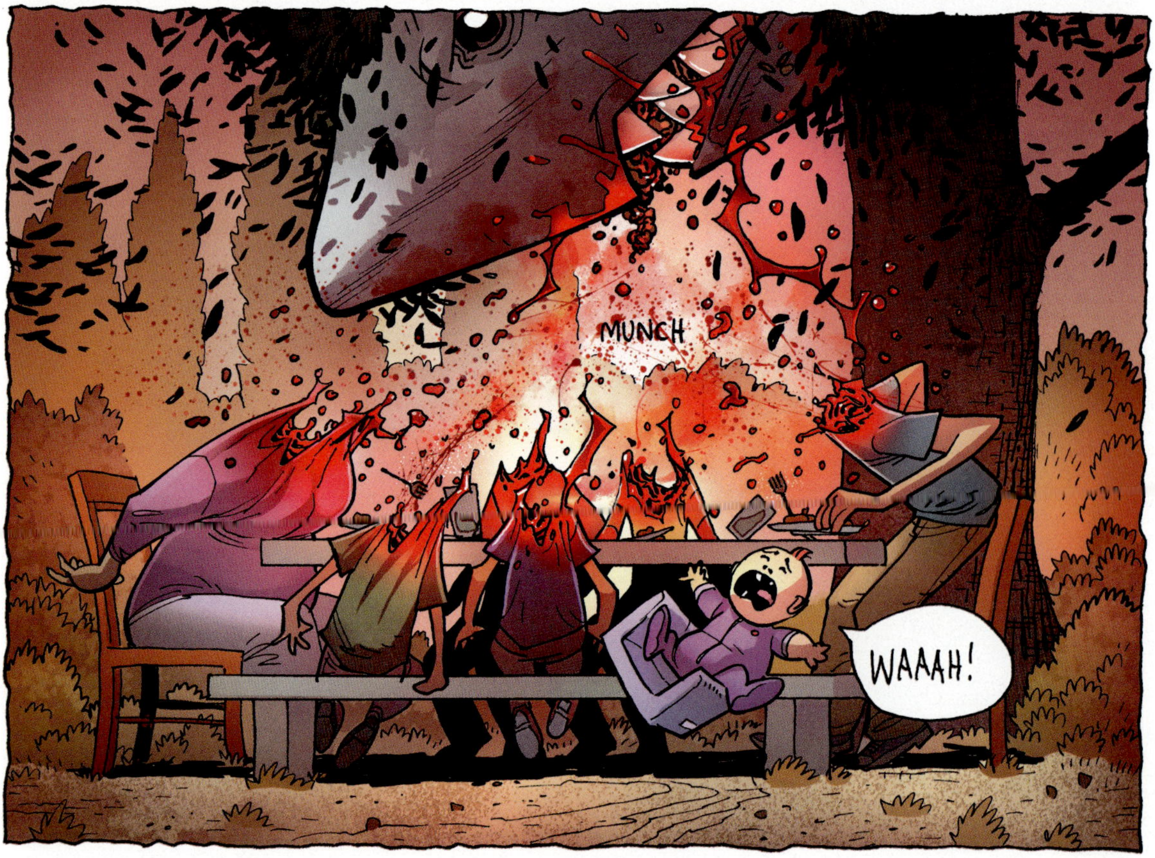
MUNCH
WAAAH!

I THOUGHT A NICE BRISK WALK WOULD HELP WITH THE BLOATING BUT IT'S ACTUALLY MAKING MY CRAMPS WORSE!
SIGH.
SOMETIMES I JUST CAN'T WAIT UNTIL MENOPAUSE, RIGHT SUSAN?
HAHA HA!

MUNCH

AGGH!!!
NOT AGAIN!
HEY CUT YOURSELF All YOU WANT, AS LONG AS YOU ARE WITH US AND OUR CINNAMON BEAR JUBILEE SHARK REPELLANT THEN YOU GOTS NO WORRIES!
RAIN
OH FU...
DON'T WORRY, I DOUBT SHARKS CAN SMELL THROUGH WATER.
LET'S GET TO HIGH GROUND AT THE TOPS OF THESE TREES TO FIND OUR BEARING. CABIN SHOULD BE CLOSE RIGHT?
I DON'T DO CLIMBING. TAKE CARL.

WELL? SEE THE CABIN?
NO, BUT I...
SHARK...
SAY AGAIN?
SHA...
HOLY DAMMIT CHRISTMAS!
MUNCH

GRRRR
RUN!
*

GAH!!!
TRIP
DAD YOU DICK! YOU LEFT ME FOR DEAD!
SON!!! YOU'RE ALIVE!? I'M SORRY DONNIE, I... LISTEN PAL...
WHEN THIS IS ALL OVER WITH I'LL BUY YOU A NEW PAIR OF PANTS, EH?
HA HA!!!
NO! DON'T YOU DARE!!
YOU'RE GONNA DIE HERE, I'LL MAKE SURE OF THAT!
THROW
HIT
OW! DAMMIT DONNIE! WHAT GIVES?
MUNCH

EAT ME FISHY!!!
SLICE
YOU MADE CARL DEAD.
RAWR
I MAKE DEAD OF YOU!
STAB

RAWR!
I MISS CARL!
I MISS CARL!
I MISS CARL!
I... OH. Hi CARL.

HEY THERE JONBOBBY. TIME TO GO HOME OK?
OKAY. YES.
HEY WOULD YOU MIND CARRYING ME?
THANKS! MY FEET WERE KILLING ME.
HA HA HA HA
HA HA HA HA

GRIZZLYSHARK
RETURNS
R. OTTLEY
+fco

IF THEY WERE TO EVER FIGHT, I'M PRETTY SURE A SHARK WOULD KILL A BEAR, LIKE EASILY.
NO WAY MAN! YOU EVER BEEN MAULED TO DEATH BY A BEAR?! TRUST ME, IT AIN'T FUN.
WHATEVER. LET'S AGREE TO DISAGREE.
YOU'RE STILL WAY WRONG THOUGH.
HEY MY OWIE STILL HURTS. CAN YOU BLOW ON IT SOME MORE?
SURE THING, FRIEND.

I DON'T WANT CANCER IN MY KNEE!
BLOW ME WITH GOOD AIR!
OH MY OMG!!!
MUNCH
MUNCH
MUNCH
GRIZZLY-SHARK

MEANWHILE...
A CAR! AND IT'S STOPPING! WE'RE SAVED JONBOB!
WHAT HAPPENED TO YOU BOYS?!
HELLO!
IT WAS TERRIBLE! WE WERE ATTACKED BY...
WE ATE ICE CREAM!
ATTACKED?! BY WHAT?
BAD FISHY!

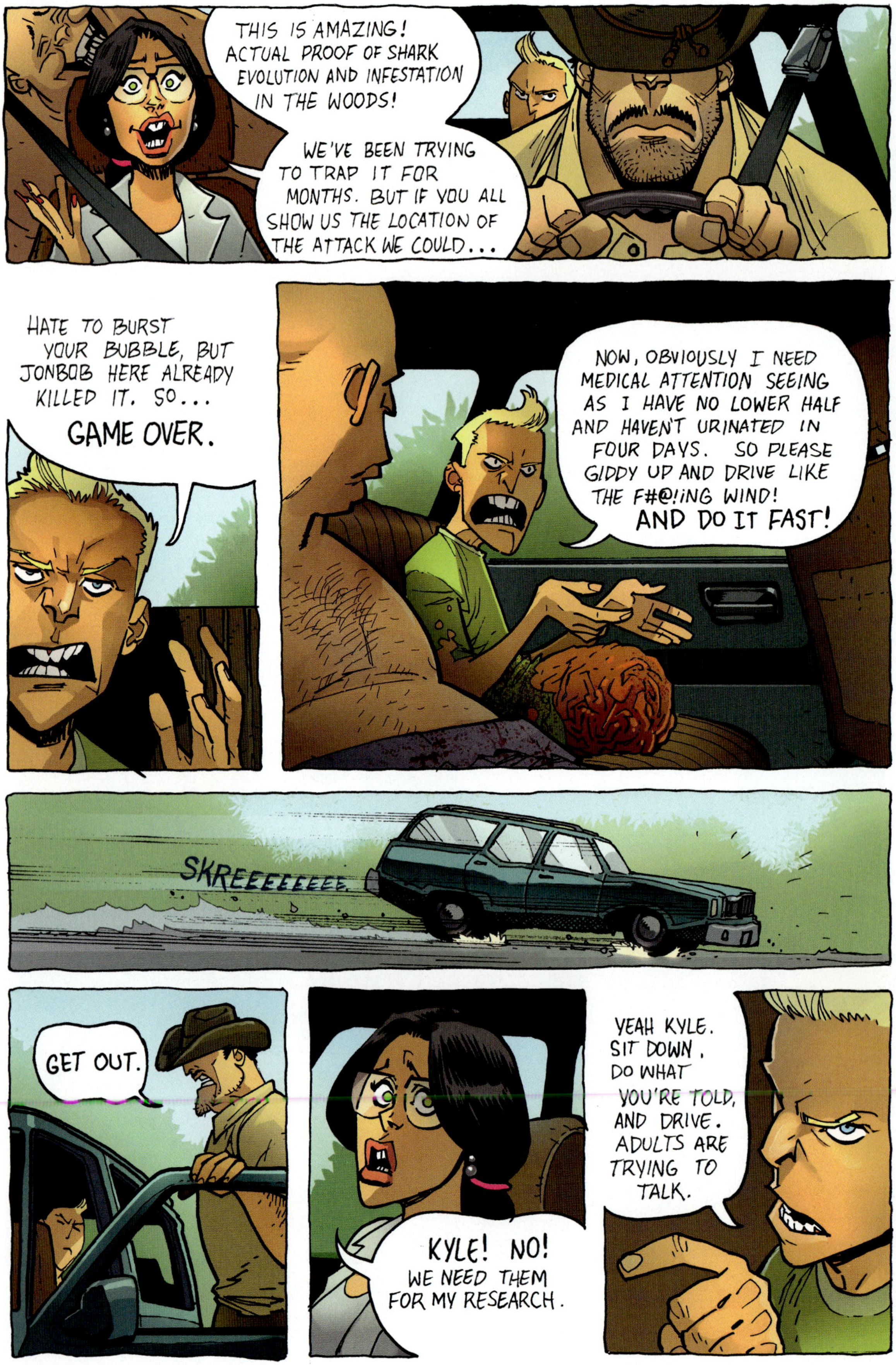
THIS IS AMAZING! ACTUAL PROOF OF SHARK EVOLUTION AND INFESTATION IN THE WOODS!
WE'VE BEEN TRYING TO TRAP IT FOR MONTHS. BUT IF YOU ALL SHOW US THE LOCATION OF THE ATTACK WE COULD...
HATE TO BURST YOUR BUBBLE, BUT JONBOB HERE ALREADY KILLED IT. SO... GAME OVER.
NOW, OBVIOUSLY I NEED MEDICAL ATTENTION SEEING AS I HAVE NO LOWER HALF AND HAVEN'T URINATED IN FOUR DAYS. SO PLEASE GIDDY UP AND DRIVE LIKE THE F#@!ING WIND! AND DO IT FAST!
SKREEEEEEEEE.
GET OUT.
KYLE! NO! WE NEED THEM FOR MY RESEARCH.
YEAH KYLE. SIT DOWN. DO WHAT YOU'RE TOLD, AND DRIVE. ADULTS ARE TRYING TO TALK.

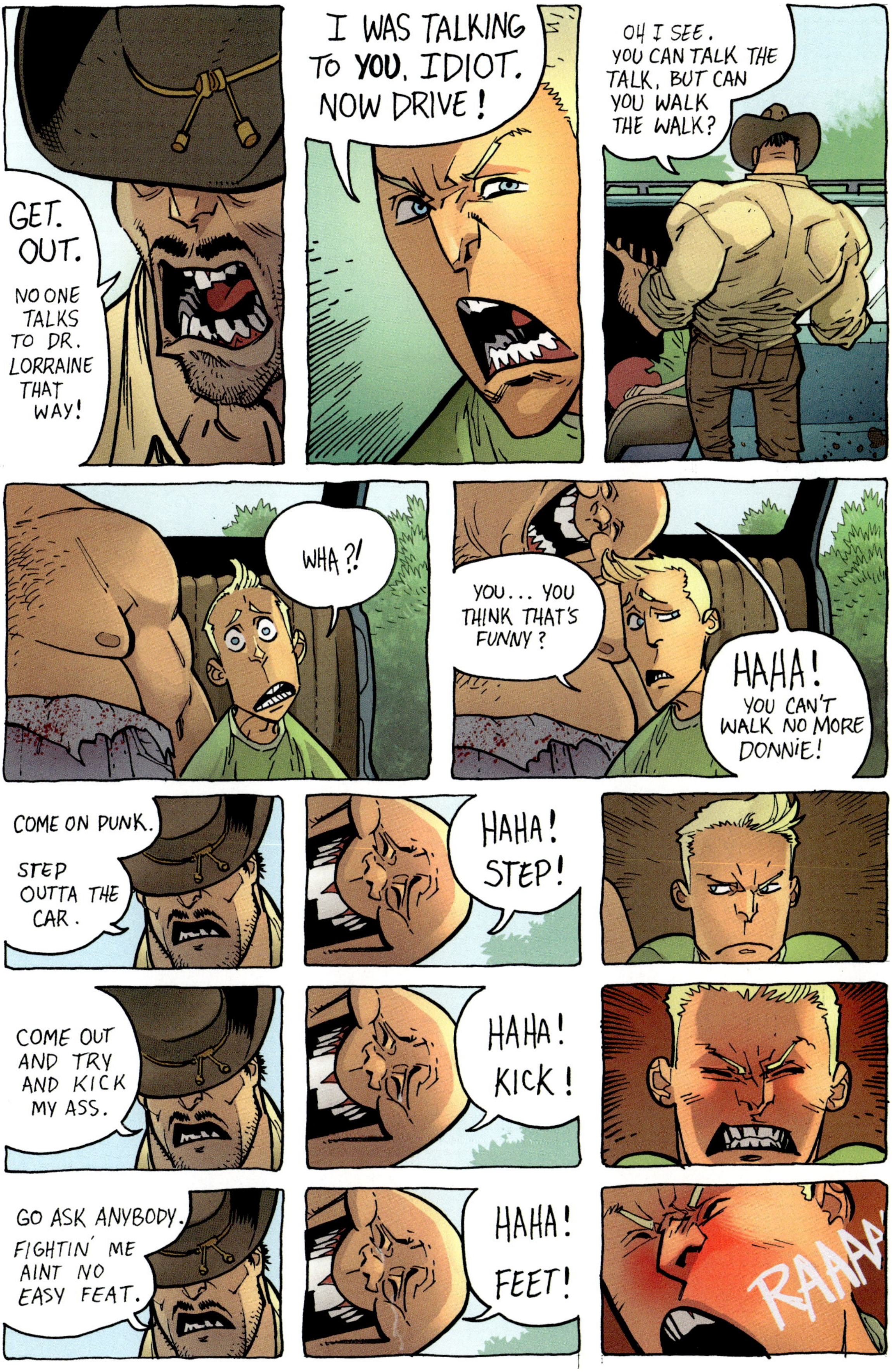
GET. OUT.
NO ONE TALKS TO DR. LORRAINE THAT WAY!
I WAS TALKING TO YOU, IDIOT. NOW DRIVE!
OH I SEE. YOU CAN TALK THE TALK, BUT CAN YOU WALK THE WALK?
WHA?!
YOU... YOU THINK THAT'S FUNNY?
HAHA! YOU CAN'T WALK NO MORE DONNIE!
COME ON PUNK.
STEP OUTTA THE CAR.
HAHA! STEP!
COME OUT AND TRY AND KICK MY ASS.
HAHA! KICK!
GO ASK ANYBODY.
FIGHTIN' ME AINT NO EASY FEAT.
HAHA! FEET!
RAAA

AAAAAAAAA! IT BURNS!
HA HA! BURN!
GAH!
YOU'RE DEAD FREAK!
DON'T TOUCH MY DONNIE.
PUSH
SLAM
GAAAAH!
KYLE!

YOU CHOSE POORLY, KYLE. NEXT TIME YOU'LL DO YOUR DAMN JOB.
CLICK
VRRMMMM
STOP!
STOP IT!
STOP!
THUMP
SKREEEEEECH
RIIIIIIIP
GAAAAAAAHH

1 MILE AWAY
GRRRRrrr
RUSTLE
RUSTLE
VOOOOOOOOOOOOSH

RAWR

OH NO!
HOW?!
HAHA! YOU DRIVE SO BUMPY!

FOLLOW IT IN THE WOODS!
THUNK
VRRRROOO
NO! ARE YOU CRAZY? I'M NOT GOING NEAR THAT THING!
THUNK
SCREEEEECH
KYLE NEEDS OUR HELP!
JONBOB! I NEED HELP!
BUT. . . HE'S A GIRL. I DON'T HIT THOSE.
THIS COULD BE WORTH MILLIONS IF WE CATCH ONE!
OH.
OK.

We didn't find Kyle the driver or the shark that day.
We did find a child stranded in a picnic location, family destroyed by a feral wood shark.
Survived only by feeding on entrails of parents.
SHARK BUSTERS™
Dr. Lorraine made me some awesome pants, with new legs!
I love her.

Jonbob Loves her too. But come on, he doesn't stand a chance with anyone.

Shark traps are set and ready to Go.
Dr. Lorraine's theory is there might be more than one Shark and they've gotten a taste for human flesh. so, that could be why we aren't attracting them to the traps.
She teases me and says my Lower half must have been delicious.
I Love her.
I miss my Lower half and wish I could show it to her.
I hope we catch that shark soon before anyone else gets hurt.

SOWWY DADDY!
NO! I TOLD YOU NOT TO PLAY WITH THAT.
NOW GO TO YOUR TIME-OUT CHAIR.
NO! I DON'T WANNA!
MUNCH

COME ON DARLIN'. YA CAN'T SPEND THE REST OF OUR HONEYMOON SULKING OVER A LITTLE BLOODY NOSE!
IF IT MAKES YOU FEEL ANY BETTER, MY KNUCKLES BROKE SKIN TOO.

MUNCH
MUNCH

HOLD UP, TROOP! I JUST SWATTED A MOSQUITO. TIME TO BREAK OUT THE INSECT REPELLENT.
SHEESH. THAT THING WAS SUCKING ME DRY.
LIKE YOUR MOM.
HEY!
I GOTTA PEE.

MUNCH

WE GOT ONE! LOCATION 4 TRAP WAS SET OFF! LET'S GO!
SHARK BUSTERS!
!
WHA?! HE'S STILL ALIVE?!
DAMMIT.

NO! WAIT!
IT'S A TRAP!
WELL NO DUH IT'S A TRAP, YOU AND I BUILT IT.
NO, THE SHARK IS WAITING FOR YOU IN THE GRASS!
WOOOOOOOSH

PLEASE GET BACK IN THE CAR!
NOT WITHOUT YOU!
ROAR
SNAP
NO MORE EATING OF PEOPLE.

SLAM
EAT OF DIRT.
NOW EAT OF SOME ROCKS! HA HA HA!
KRAK
ROAR

NO MELISSA, HE ACTUALLY DUMPED ME!
YEAH, I WAS A COMPLETE MESS. I MEAN SERIOUSLY, I'VE NEVER BEEN MORE CRUSHED.
THOOM
LICK LICK
BARK BARK
LICK LICK

PUNCH IT IN THE NOSE! THEY HATE THAT!
JONBOB'S MOM ALWAYS SAID HE WAS SPECIAL.
NOW I SEE WHY!

THERE'S TOO MANY!!
SON OF A DAMMIT.
GAME OVER, MAN!

GRIZZLYSHARK
VS.
SEABEAR

:EBOOK UPDATE STATUS
POST
DRIVING IN WOODS. GUY IS TOTALLY CHECKING ME OUT. SO WEIRD. I DIDN'T EVEN PUT ON MAKEUP TODAY! :)
CLICK CLICK CLICK CLICK
ITTER
TWEET
ROWDYKEVINLADYLUVR2000
@KEVINISREVINFORYORBOD
GIRLZ LOOK SO DUM WITHOUT MAKEUP, AMIRITE GUYS? LOL #STOOPIDGIRLZ #FML
CLICK CLICK CLICK CLICK
CRASH
BARK BARK
MUNCH
MUNCH
MEANWHILE...
CRAP! HOW MANY ARE THERE?!?

MEANWHILE....
NEW MESSAGE FROM:
ROSALYNN
TODAY
HEY SEXY MAN, JUST THINKING ABOUT 9/11 AND WANT YOU TO DRIVE EXTRA SAFE TODAY. CAN'T IMAGINE LOSING YOU! ACTUALLY I HOPE YOU WAIT AND READ THIS WHEN YOU ARE NOT DRIVING. WE ALL KNOW HOW SLOW YOU READ. LOL. HMMM... MAYBE I SHOULD JUST SEND THIS LATER DURING YOUR LUNCH BREAK. NO, I DON'T WANT TO RE-TYPE IT. OK BE SAFE AND REMEMBER TO READ THIS LATER, OK? LUV YA LOTS, HONEY POT!
WATCH OUT!
SCREEEEECH!
SCREEEEEEEEEEE...
SLAM
MEANWHILE...
WAIT! WHERE ARE THEY GOING?!

MUNCH

HURRY! WHILE THEY'RE GONE! I HAVE AN IDEA!
WE NEED TO GET THEM NEAR A CLIFF. I THINK WE CAN LURE THEM WITH BAIT RIGHT OFF A LEDGE! WE CAN KILL THEM ALL IN ONE SHOT!
NOW YOU'RE TALKIN! GREAT IDEA! LET'S GET TO IT!
SO GLAD YOU ARE BACK. I'M SO SICK OF DRIVING!
OH. RIGHT.
DON'T WORRY KYLE. I CAN DRIVE. FROM NOW ON... I'LL BE YOUR HANDS!
YOU HEAR ME? I'LL **BE** YOUR HANDS, KYLE!
I GOTTA PEE.
I DON'T WANT TO BE YOUR HANDS ANYMORE.

MUNCH
LORRAINE!!!
NO!
FLY, YOU FOOLS!
DAMMIT!

SIT ON THE ACCELERATOR AND DON'T MOVE!
VRRRRMMMMM
WAIT!
STOP! LET ME IN, MAN!
NO! YOU LET LORRAINE DIE! YOU SHOULD HAVE SAVED HER. BUT NO, YOU JUST STOOD THERE AND LET HER TOUCH YOUR FACE. AND.. AND... DID SHE LIKE YOU?!
NO! SHE...SHE'S DEAD.
AND NOW SO ARE YOU!

VRRRRMMMMMMMMM...
NO!!
MUNCH
SPLAT!
ONE DOWN. THE REST TO GO!

LATER...
THIS BAIT SUCKS.
WE HAVEN'T LURED ANYTHING IN DAYS. WE'RE DOING SOMETHING WRONG.

JUST PULL THE BAIT IN ALREADY.
FWWIPP
KRAK
NOT SO HARD!
CRAP! THE ROPE IS STUCK.
NOW I GOTTA GO OUT AND GET IT!
WHAT THE HELL ARE YOU DOING?!

I SAVE YOU, DONNIE.
?

RAWR
GAH!

MUNCH
SNAP

R. OTTLEY
iplx!

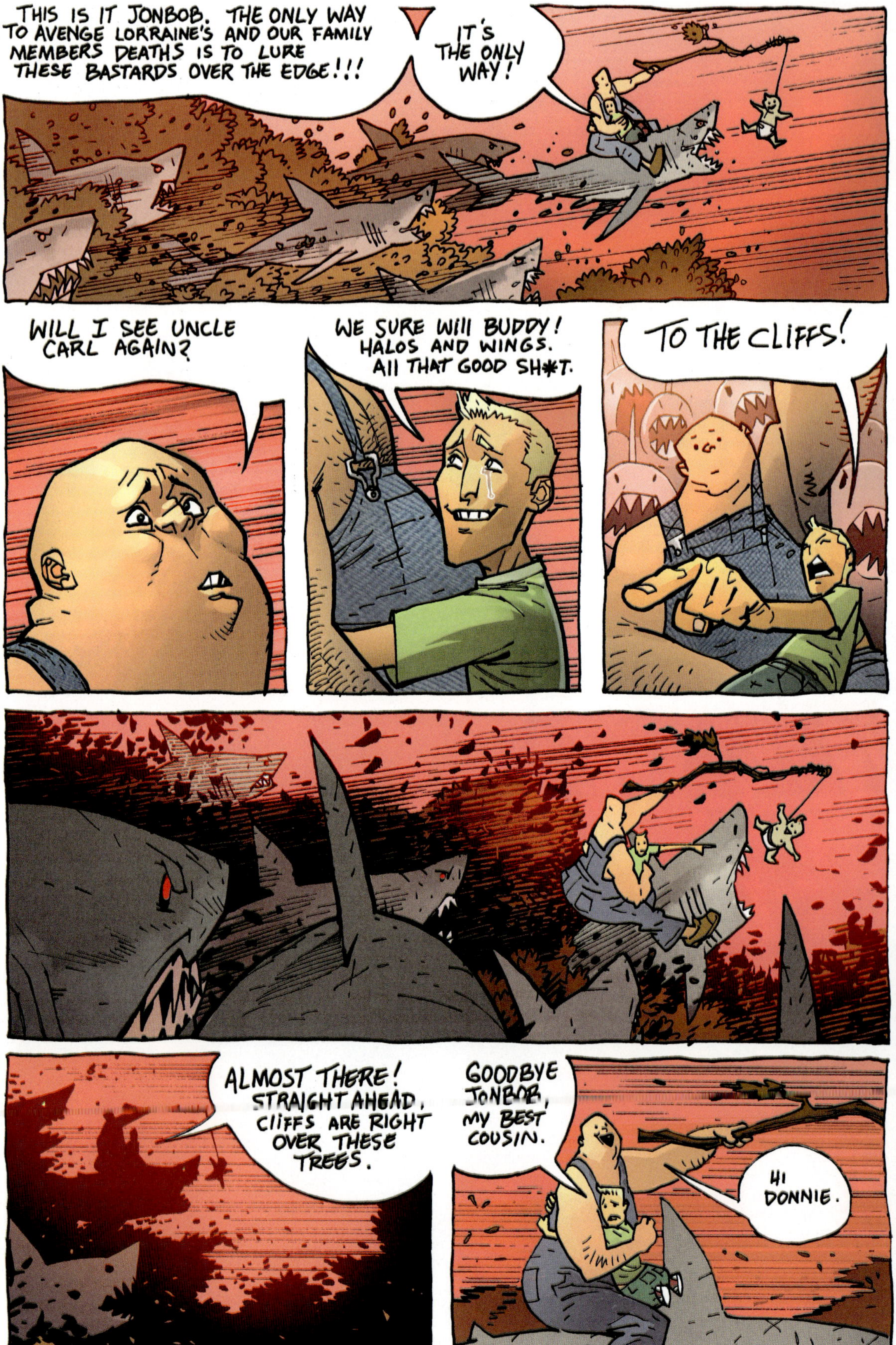
THIS IS IT JONBOB. THE ONLY WAY TO AVENGE LORRAINE'S AND OUR FAMILY MEMBERS DEATHS IS TO LURE THESE BASTARDS OVER THE EDGE!!!
IT'S THE ONLY WAY!
WILL I SEE UNCLE CARL AGAIN?
WE SURE WILL BUDDY! HALOS AND WINGS. ALL THAT GOOD SH*T.
TO THE CLIFFS!
ALMOST THERE! STRAIGHT AHEAD, CLIFFS ARE RIGHT OVER THESE TREES.
GOODBYE JONBOB, MY BEST COUSIN.
HI DONNIE.

DON'T LOOK, JONBOB.
DON'T...
OH SH*T BALLS.

SPLOOSH
WE STILL ALIVE, DONNIE!
COUGH COUGH
CRAP! NOT FOR LONG! WE'RE ON THEIR TURF NOW. WE LOST!
WE FAILED. WE... WAIT!

THEY'RE DROWNING?! HAHAH!
DONNIE, LOOKIE.
OH NO. ANOTHER ONE!
GRRRRR
HEY COME ON IN! THE WATER IS DELICIOUS!
HE'S TOO SMART! HE'S JUST ONE SHARK THOUGH, YOU CAN KILL IT, RIGHT?
THATS A SCARY BIG FISHY, DONNIE. NO WAY. NUH-UH.
UH... PLEASE TELL ME THAT WAS YOU.
POP GURGLE

GRRRRR
???
BUNNY?
ROAR

THOOM
RAWR
SHUFFLE SHUFFLE
PAF
SMACK
ROAR

OH COME ON, SEA BEAR! YOU GOTTA DO MORE THAN JUST ROAR AT IT! KILL IT!!
SORRY. YOU'RE DOING FINE. HE WENT THAT WAY THOUGH.
GRAB
THROW
YES! INTO THE WATER! HAHA!
THUMP

!
UGH! HOW DO YOU MISS THE OCEAN?!
STUPID ASS BEARS.
SPLOOSH
DAD? THERE'S A SHARK!
IT'S OK, SON. SHARKS CAN'T GET US IN HERE.
OK DAD, I GOT THE GUN!
WHAT? NO!
GUNS ARE VERY DANGEROUS! AND...
RAAAR
NO! MY WORST NIGHTMARE!
DAD! NO!

DAMMIT, SON! LET ME DIE!
NO! WE CAN MAKE IT THROUGH THIS.
BLAM
SEE?! WHAT DID I TELL YOU? GUNS ARE VERY DANGEROUS! YOU COULD'VE KILLED ME!
SORRY, DAD.
WOW, IT'S BLEEDING LIKE CRAZY!
DROOL
PUSH
SPLOOSH
MUNCH
VRMMMMMMMM

THOOM
WOOSH
RAWRRR

ROAR
FWOOSH
SMACK
HURRY! LETS GET OUT OF HERE WHILE THEY'RE DISTRACTED.
WHOA! THE BEAR HAS THE UPPER HAND! LUCKY FOR US HE SHOWED UP.
GO SEA BEAR!
?

MUNCH
YEESH! OK, RUN. RUN!
GRRRRRRR...
NOW WHAT DONNIE?
NOW? NOW WE DIE.
GRRRR
OK.
GULP
WHY'D YOU DO THAT?!

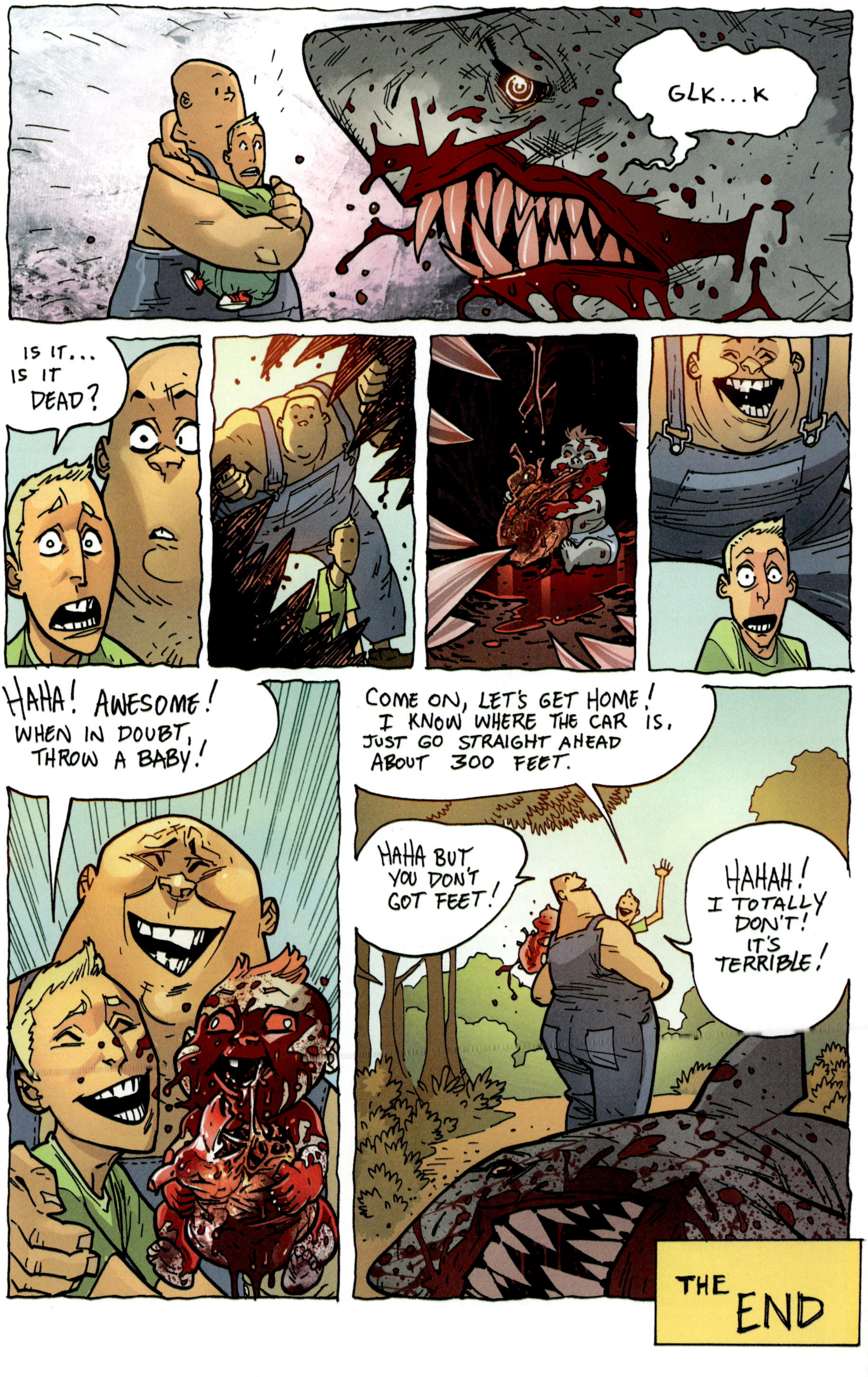
GLK...K
IS IT... IS IT DEAD?
HAHA! AWESOME! WHEN IN DOUBT, THROW A BABY!
COME ON, LET'S GET HOME! I KNOW WHERE THE CAR IS. JUST GO STRAIGHT AHEAD ABOUT 300 FEET.
HAHA BUT YOU DON'T GOT FEET!
HAHAH! I TOTALLY DON'T! IT'S TERRIBLE!
THE END

GRIZZLY PROCESS

It means a lot that you would take a chance on a book called GRIZZLYSHARK. I love hearing how much laughter this book has caused someone, because in the end, that's really all I wanted out of this book, to make myself laugh, then to make you laugh. If you don't laugh, you may return this book to any comic store. Not for a refund, but so they can sell it to someone else who could use it. Hey, comic shop dudes gotta eat. So thank you for reading! I think I love you. *Read on!*

There're bonus features on the *Snow White* DVD where they talk about how Walt Disney sent out a memo to all the artists and told them he'd pay 5 dollars for any Dwarf gags that made it into the film. Now, for someone like me, I would've been all over that -- well, maybe for more than 5 dollars, but still. I like stupid, silly gag cartoons; I was raised on *Looney Tunes, Mad Magazine*, and newspaper comic strips. I didn't get into comic books until I was 15, but I loved making funny gags, so when this crazy idea of a bear and a shark getting mixed up came about, I took it as a chance to play with some of the insanity that's been locked away in my head for a while. Even though I don't have much experience as a writer, I wanted to give it a go. Basically, I started writing with a brainstorm of what I wanted to see, what I thought would be funny. Then some gags got eliminated, and some I kept, made bigger, and I'd think of more ideas and figure out how to tie them all together into a somewhat coherent story. It was extremely fun making this book. I will show you scans of how I wrote this book in this section. Gags that got dropped and the ones I kept, you'll see my rough thumbnail sketches where a lot of the dialogue and writing happened. And some of the earliest sketches, covers, and origins of this book! ***Lets do this!***

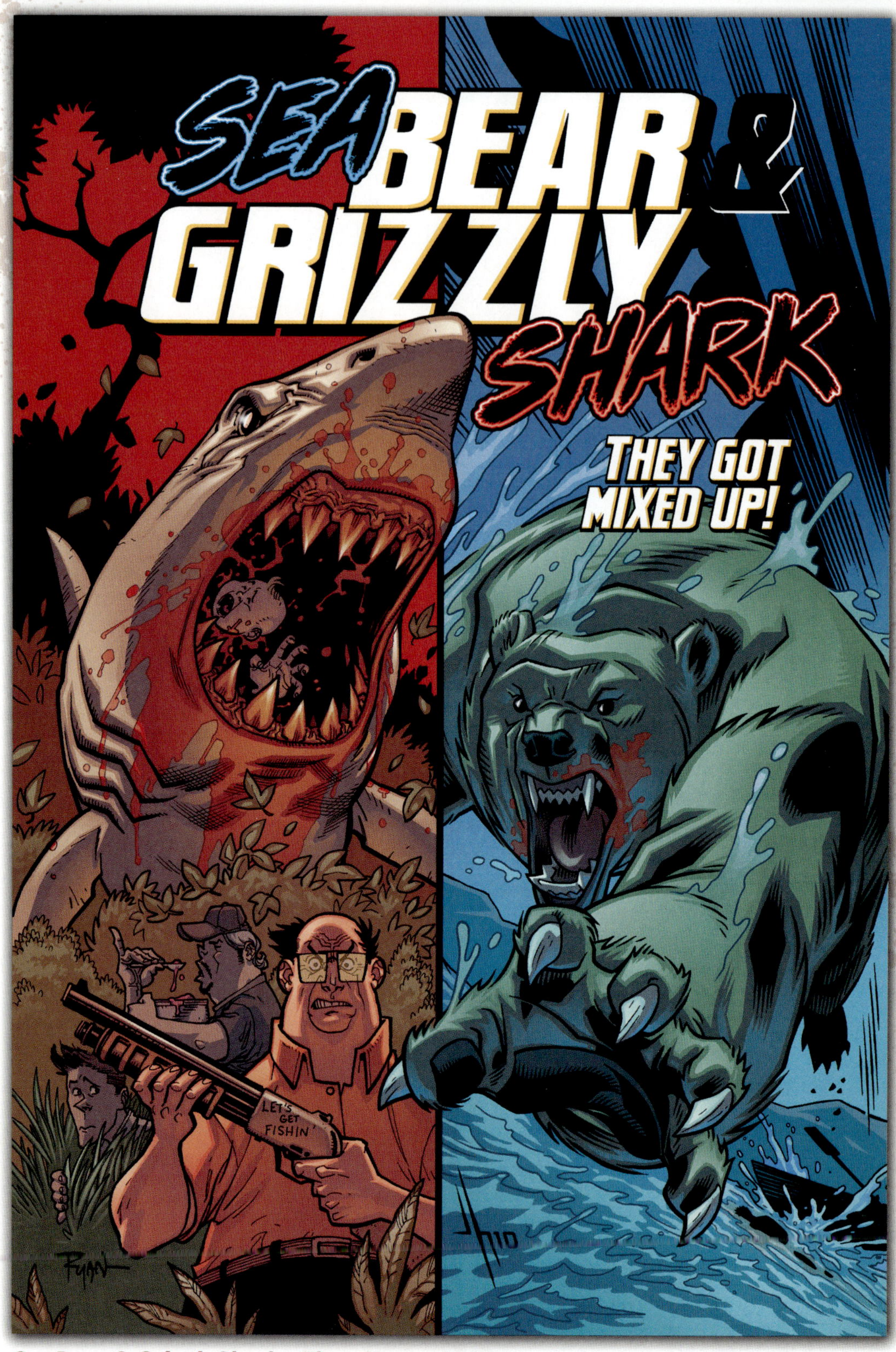

***SeaBear & GrizzlyShark* - First Cover, 2010**

This is the book that started it all back in 2010. *SeaBear & GrizzlyShark!* It all happened because my good friend Jason Howard and I were drunk on fatigue and coming up with stupid ideas after a long day at a comic convention one year, and we hit on one idea about a bear and a shark getting mixed up. And from then on we were hooked. We both wanted to try out the 24 Hour Comic thing, so we decided this was the idea we would do. Now 24 Hour Comic Day is a day where many crazy artists feel like staying up 24 hours straight and create an entire comic: writing, art, lettering, all of it! It's an insane exercise. I've done it a few times, and it breaks my brain every time! So our idea was that I would take the shark, Jason would take the bear, and we'd do our own separate books in 24 hours. Well, we didn't make it. These are NOT official 24 hour comics. But close. I managed to write all of my issue of *GrizzlyShark* and draw 10 pages completely. Then, in between pages of *Invincible,* I'd work on *GrizzlyShark* here and there.

First Sketch

This is the first sketch I made after I got home from that comic con where Jason and I came up with this idea.

I treated it like an ad, and then I made a couple more before we finally made our issues.

COME ON IN, THE WATER IS FANTASTICAlly DELICIOUS!
NO WAY! I'M AFRAID OF BEARS.
RYAN

SeaBear & GrizzlyShark - Second Printing Cover, 2010

The first issue ended up selling out, it was a cult hit! So we did a reprint cover. Here's my half of the cover displaying Donnie and Jonbob and the GrizzlyShark in all their gory glory.

SeaBear half illustrated by Jason Howard, of course. Cover colors by FCO...

Kirkman Origin

So Jason and I were hanging out with our good friend and the guy who writes the books we work on, **Robert Kirkman**. We told him about our stories, and immediately he said he wanted to do a one-page origin story. He's a pretty good writer so we totally let him. This was printed in that first issue. I hope someday a future civilization will find this book and treat it like gospel. That's the plan anyway.

SEA BEAR

WRITTEN & DRAWN BY:
JASON HOWARD

GRIZZLY SHARK

WRITTEN & DRAWN BY:
RYAN OTTLEY
GRAY TONES BY CLIFF RATHBURN

THE ORIGIN OF THE BEAR, AND THE ORIGIN OF THE SHARK

An origin tale by **Robert (Robert) Kirkman**

And lo, in the time before time was time and space was space, in the remote reaches of our universe, there was the planet Earth. It was not the Earth we know today, this Earth was very much very different. What we know now to be land was not land at all. And what we know now to be water was not water... at all. What we know now as land was in fact water. And what we know now as water was in fact land. All of the land creatures we know now existed in this time and lived their lives in water. All of the water creatures we know now existed in this time and lived their lives on land. And everyone was happy.

And then came the time of the great reversal. It was a time of great calamity and upheaval. Many lives were lost in the transition and still many more lives were forever changed forever. Mountains roared and oceans cried as the massive shift took place. What we knew then to be land became water. And what we knew then to be water became land. All of the animals of Earth that lived in water were suddenly made to live on land. And all of the animals of Earth that lived on land were suddenly made to live in water. It was a time of great hardship as the great water creatures, the elephant, the wolf and the bird were forced to live on land. And it was a time of great hardship as the great land creatures, the whale, the fish and the dolphin were forced to live in water.

But poor unfortunate bear and poor unfortunate shark...

...THEY GOT MIXED UP!

GRIZZLYSHARK Volume 1 Trade Papeback Cover

I wanted more. I had so much fun making that first issue that I told Jason I wanted to do another 24 hour comic day to do a second issue. He said he was down. So I wrote and did the layouts for the entire issue 2 in 24 hours, and again, in between *Invincible* issues, I'd finish the pages. The problem was, when I wrote it, I had too much stuff to fit into one issue, so it had to be two more issues. Jason got too busy with work to do any more of his *Sea Bear,* but I kept plugging away on my *GrizzlyShark.* And after a while I finally finished and released it. This book is drenched in the most ridiculous amounts of blood I've ever made. And I've made a **lot** drawing *Invincible*. I've only had very few complaints about the violence in my books, so that means most of you are pretty sick-minded people! But that's ok, it's **happy** gore.

GRIZZLYSHARK #1 Cover

For the first issue I wanted something iconic, and nothing screams **shark** like seeing that fin rise above the water. Or in this case, the trees. This issue is basically that first issue from 2010, but now in color.

GRIZZLYSHARK #2: GRIZZLYSHARK RETURNS Cover

Sharks in the grass, reminiscent of *Jurassic Park* when the velociraptors are in the grass killing everyone. Clever girls!

GRIZZLYSHARK #3: GRIZZLYSHARK VS. SEABEAR Cover

GrizzlyShark Vs SeaBear! This was the grand finale. Where the bear finally meets the shark and has a showdown. Originally Jason Howard was going to draw the SeaBear on this cover, but again, he got too busy for good ol' SeaBear. Luckily, Jason doesn't neglect his family like he does his comic creations. Poor, abandoned SeaBear.

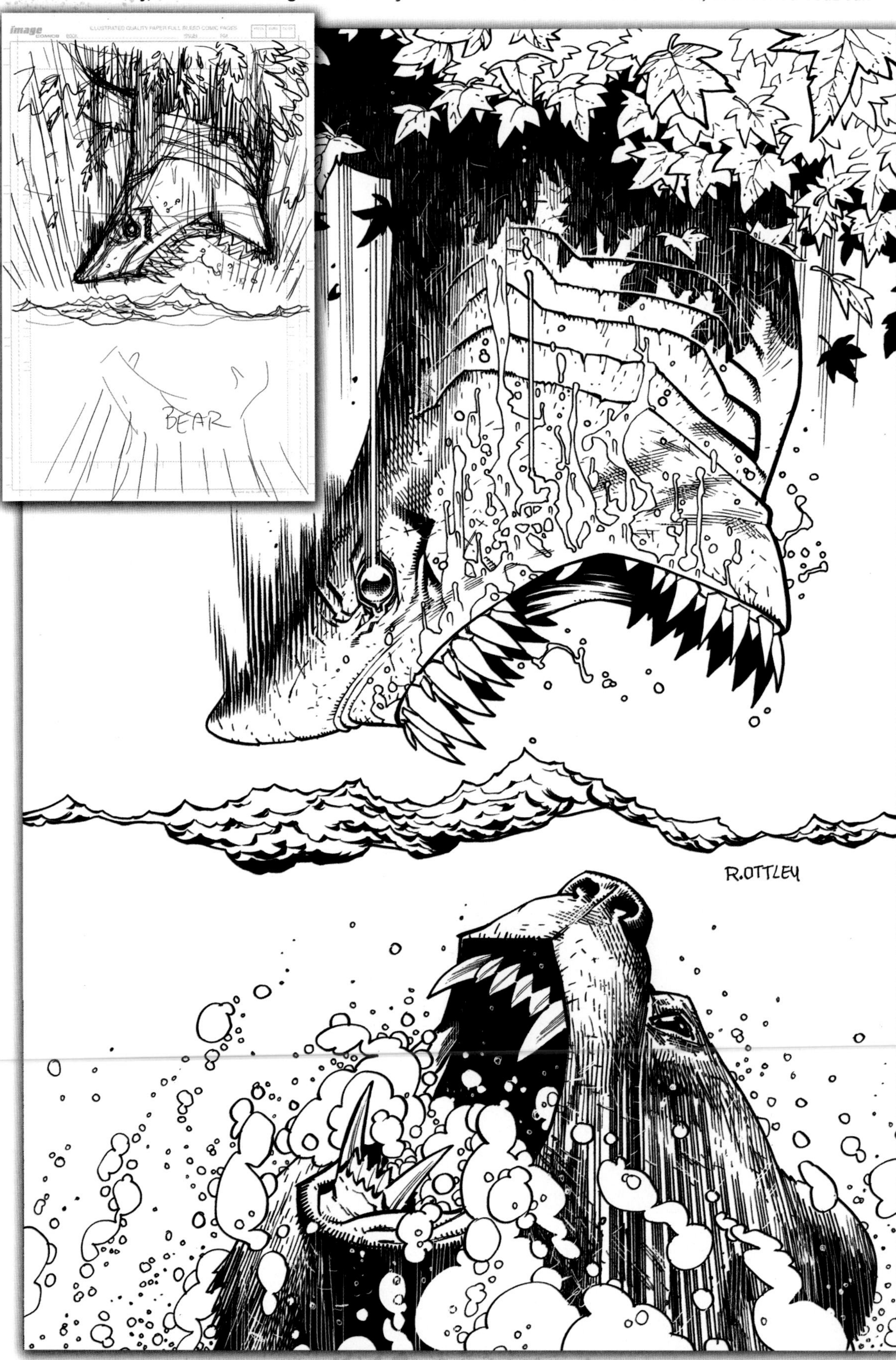

Order Code Drawing

Donnie and Jonbob doing their best to get the word out for GRIZZLYSHARK number 1.

Writing Process

Here're some scans of how I wrote this book. I wrote down all my ideas, pieced them together. A lot of times I'd write in thumbnail sketches. A lot of times I'd write down quick plot ideas then make a number of each page and put down what's happening on each page. You'll see here that I had 24 pages for this issue but it was SO dense that I had to break it up into 2 issues.

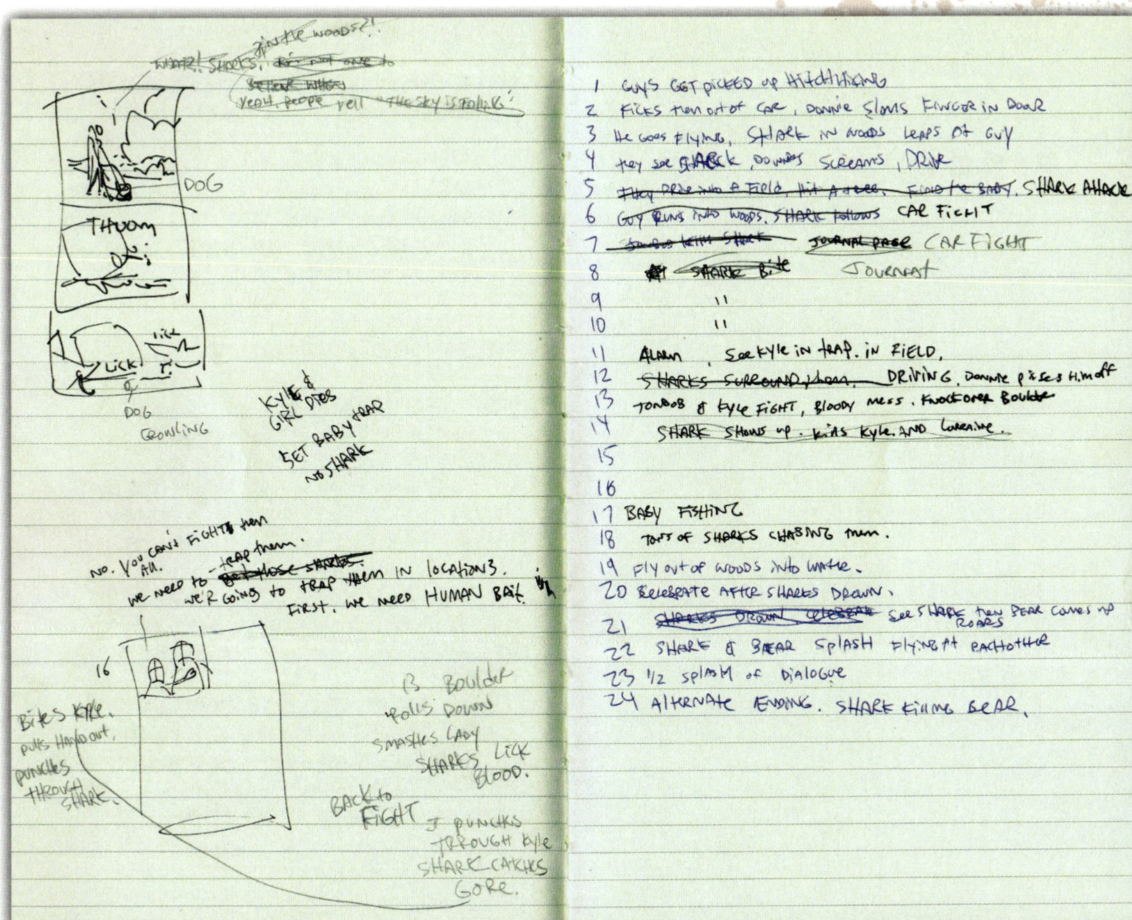

Writing Process: Issue 2

Trying to figure out the starting to issue 2 here. I still love this idea I didn't use. This "hat guy" is a real winner. Yeah, I didn't name people right away.

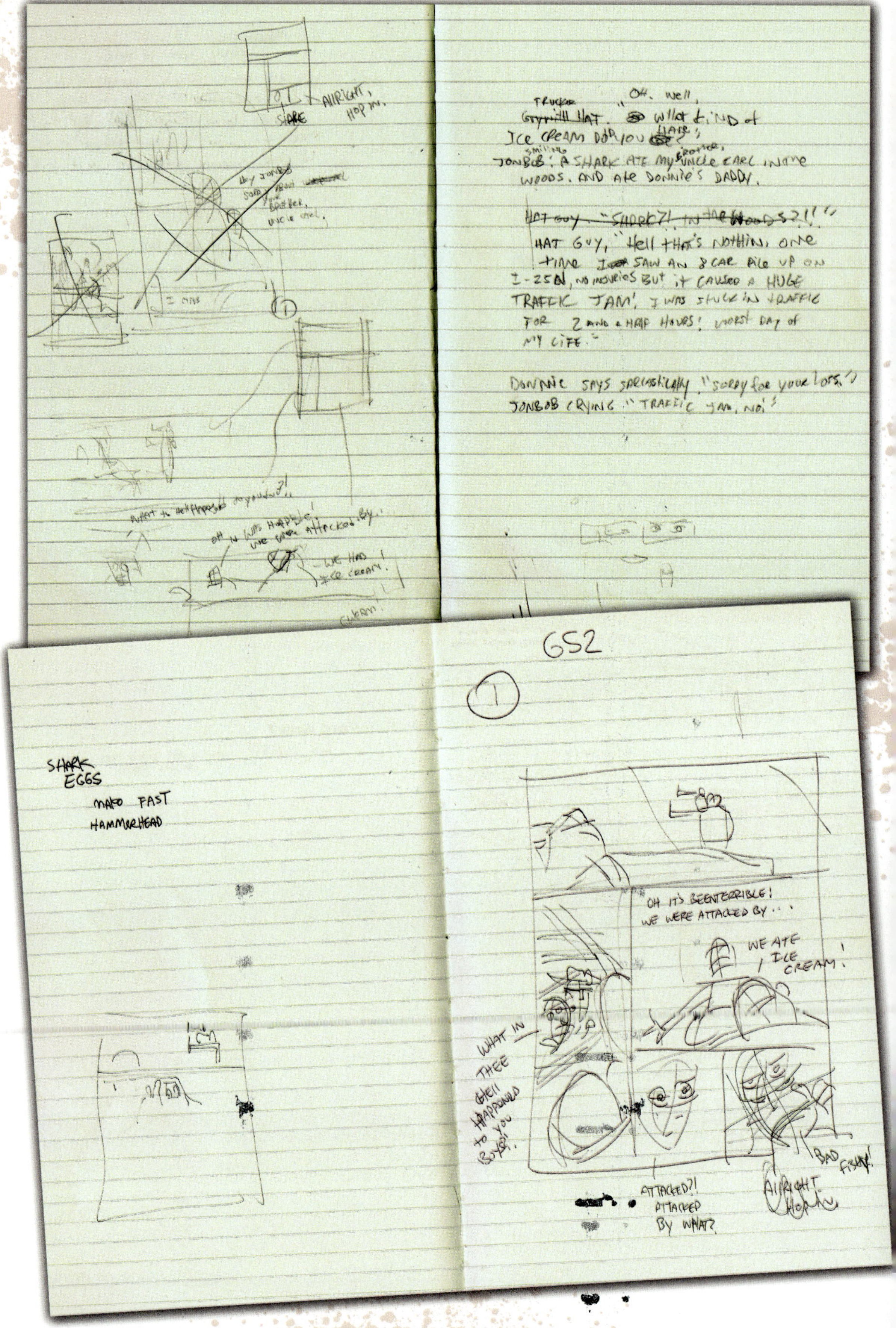

Journal Scene

The journal scene was a lot of fun to square away. Basically, I wrote down what the journal would say then did some thumbnailing to figure it all out. It's sloppy, but this kind of spastic comedy doesn't need pure refinement. My main goal was to have constant fun. It worked out!

Gag Pages

I had to do more gag pages of strangers in the forest who are bleeding -- those 3 pages from the first issue were a huge hit -- so I had to do more of those violent gags for issue 2. I didn't use this cop gag. I only wanted to show 3 strangers getting eaten gags. So here're those "Making of" pages...

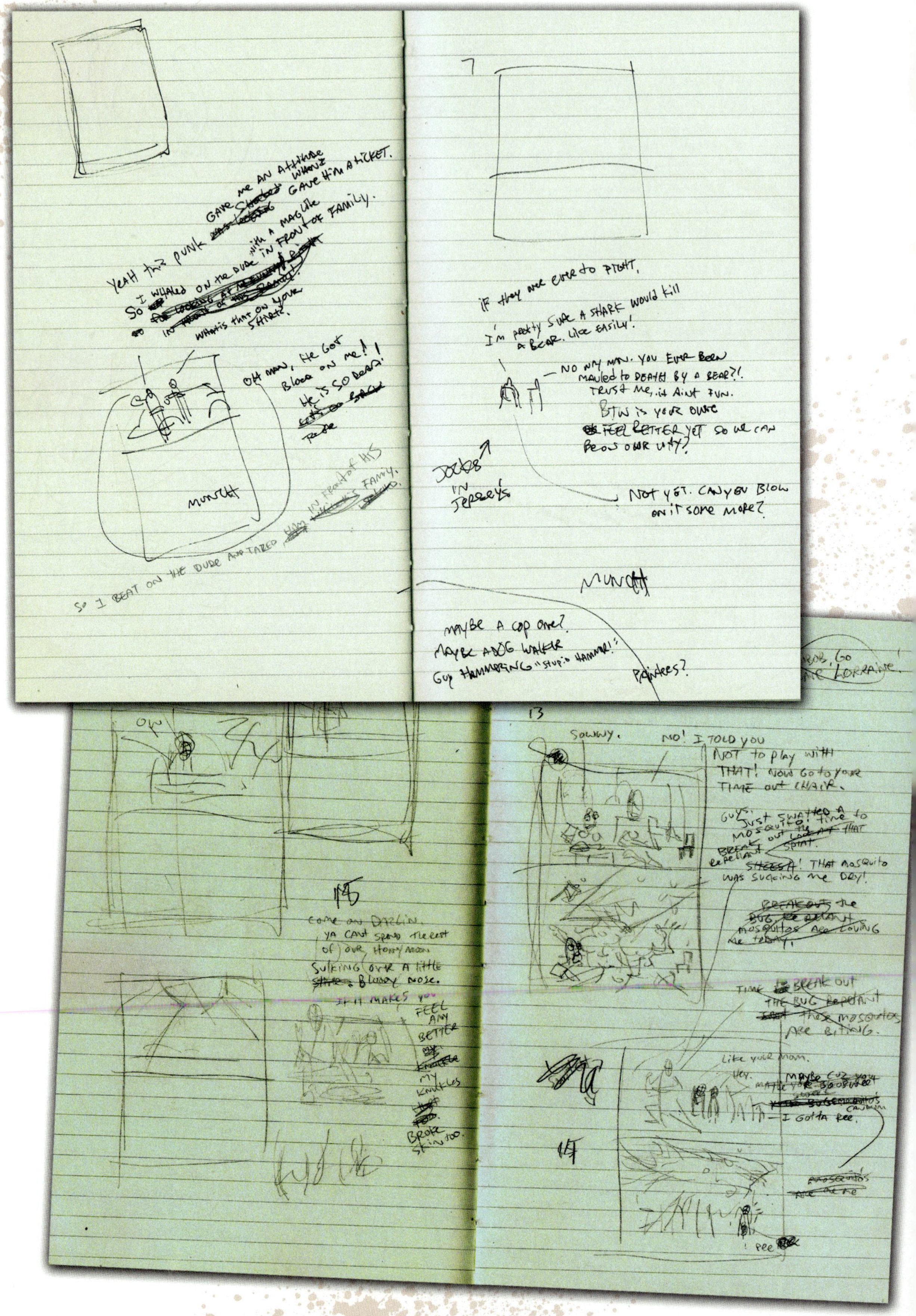

Double Page Splash

Really fun visualizing how this scene was going to work, and the double page splash was one of those pages I just couldn't wait to draw.

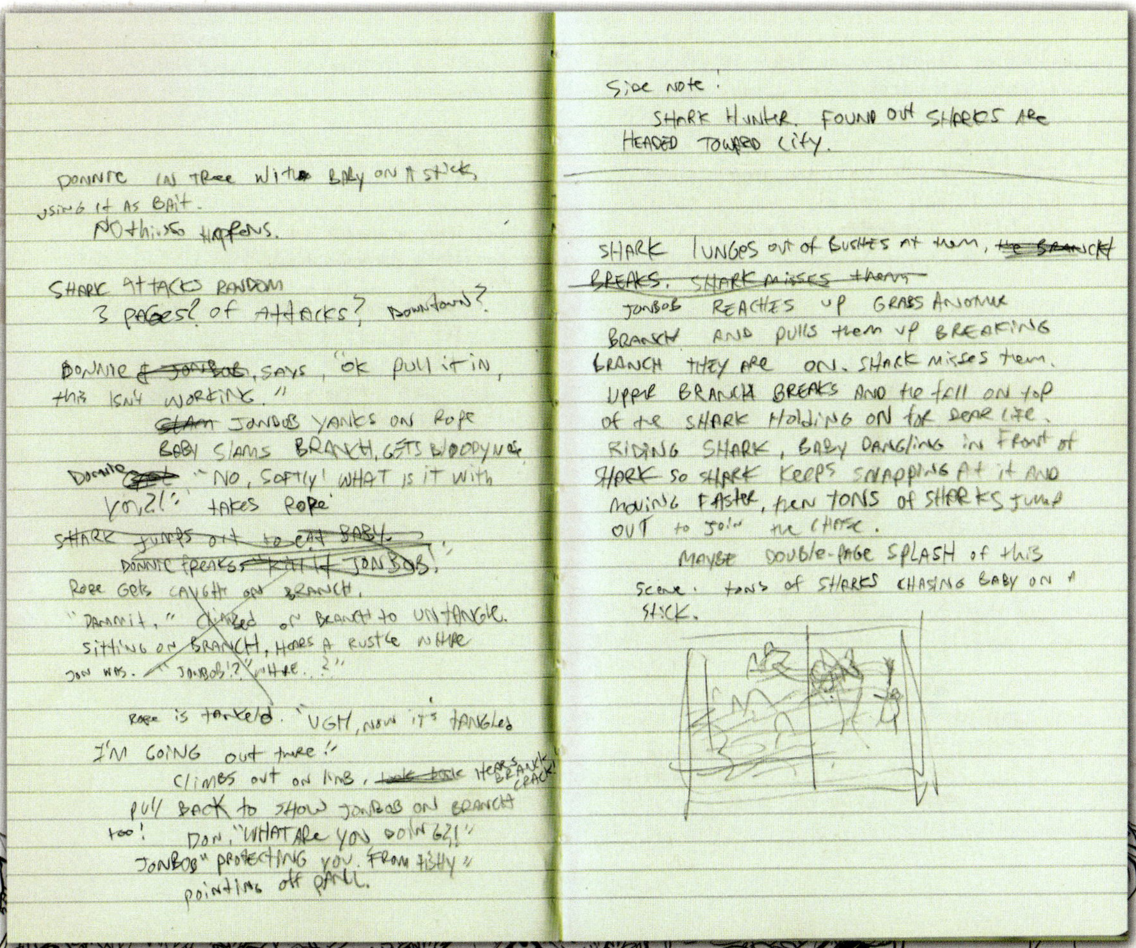

DONNIE IN TREE WITH BABY ON A STICK, USING IT AS BAIT.
NOTHING HAPPENS.

SHARK ATTACKS RANDOM
3 PAGES? OF ATTACKS? DOWNTOWN?

DONNIE ~~& JONBOB~~, SAYS, "OK PULL IT IN, THIS ISN'T WORKING."
~~SLAM~~ JONBOB YANKS ON ROPE
BABY SLAMS BRANCH, GETS BLOODY NOSE.
DONNIE: "NO, SOFTLY! WHAT IS IT WITH YOU?!" TAKES ROPE
~~SHARK JUMPS OUT TO EAT BABY.~~
~~DONNIE FREAKS, "KILL IT JONBOB!"~~
~~ROPE GETS CAUGHT ON BRANCH.~~
~~"DAMMIT," CLIMBED ON BRANCH TO UNTANGLE.~~
~~SITTING ON BRANCH, HEARS A RUSTLE WHERE JON WAS. "JONBOB!? WHERE..?"~~

ROPE IS TANKELD. "UGH, NOW IT'S TANGLED I'M GOING OUT THERE!"
CLIMBS OUT ON LIMB, ~~LOOK BACK~~ HEARS BRANCH CRACK!
PULL BACK TO SHOW JONBOB ON BRANCH TOO!
DON: "WHAT ARE YOU DOING?!"
JONBOB: "PROTECTING YOU. FROM FISHY" POINTING OFF PANEL.

SIDE NOTE:
SHARK HUNTER FOUND OUT SHARKS ARE HEADED TOWARD CITY.

SHARK LUNGES OUT OF BUSHES AT THEM, ~~THE BRANCH BREAKS. SHARK MISSES THEM~~
JONBOB REACHES UP GRABS ANOTHER BRANCH AND PULLS THEM UP BREAKING BRANCH THEY ARE ON. SHARK MISSES THEM.
UPPER BRANCH BREAKS AND THE FALL ON TOP OF THE SHARK HOLDING ON FOR DEAR LIFE.
RIDING SHARK, BABY DANGLING IN FRONT OF SHARK SO SHARK KEEPS SNAPPING AT IT AND MOVING FASTER, THEN TONS OF SHARKS JUMP OUT TO JOIN THE CHASE.
MAYBE DOUBLE-PAGE SPLASH OF THIS SCENE: TONS OF SHARKS CHASING BABY ON A STICK.

Shark V Bear

So, early on, before Jason Howard and I started working on our next 2 issues, we knew the fans wanted to see the fight between the shark and the bear, so this 3rd issue was when we wanted to give them that. But since we were writing and drawing our own issues and didn't want to interfere with each other's writing, we weren't sure how to do this. So first I thought we'd end our stories before they fought, and if you read what I wrote on that second page there you'll see what I was thinking of writing. Then the next page would simply be a drawing of the baby of the bear and the shark. Yes it's a stupid idea. But that's not why we decided against it. We decided people wanted to see them actually fight. So I said *"Alternate endings!"* We'd both do different alternate endings to the book. So in my book the shark would win, and in Jason's the bear would win. The end! It'd be perfect! But then Jason knew a bear couldn't ever beat a shark, so he went and got busy with some other project, a younger, prettier project.

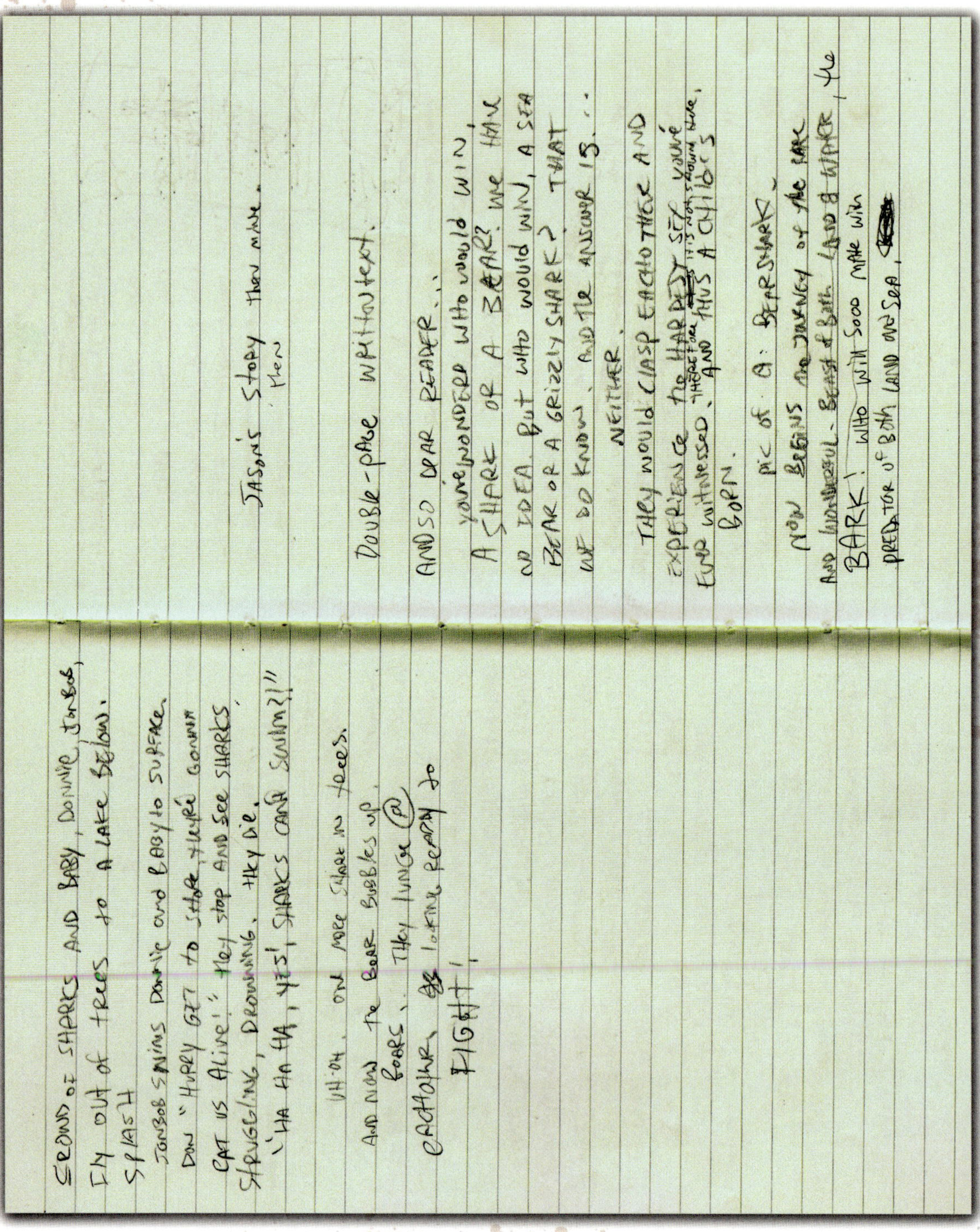

Shark V Bear, Continued

You see the pages are sectioned off, then the panels, then thumbnailing comes after this. More of the fight scene.

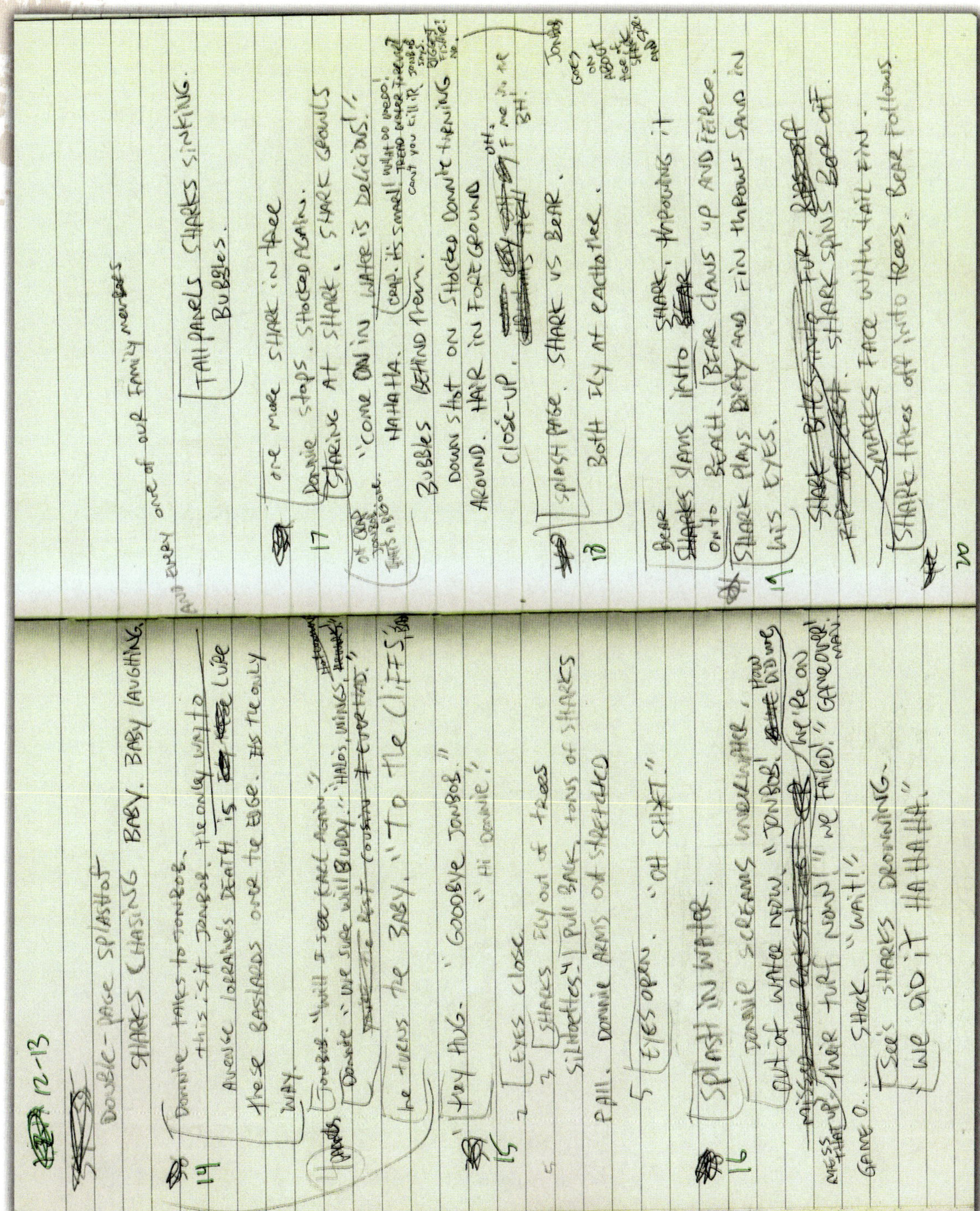

The Ending

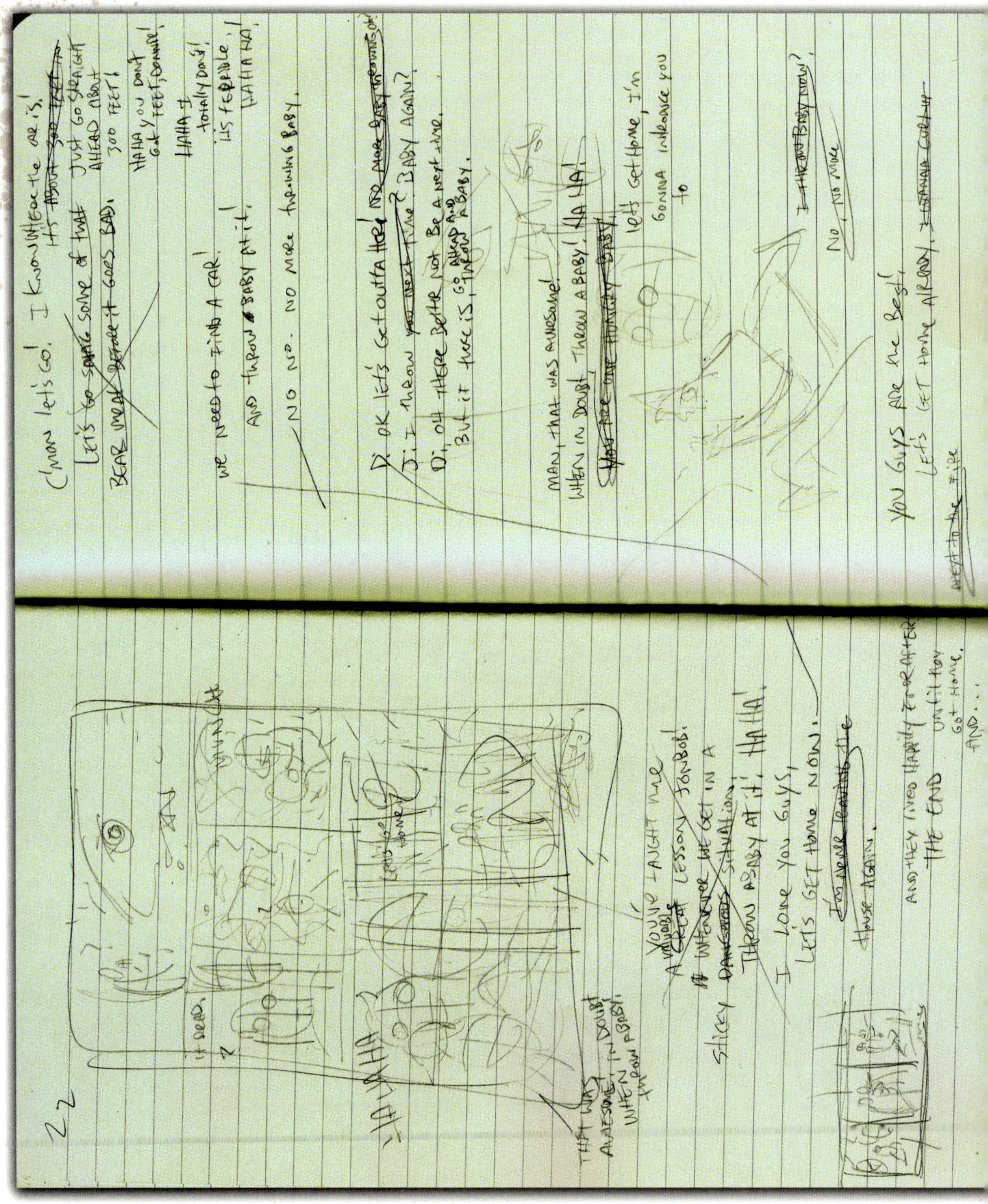

The ending where the shark dies by that crazy-ass baby was tough, because I didn't know how exactly to end it, what they would say, how it would end, etcetera. Every time I get to a point where I don't know how to go on with a story, I realize there isn't time for writer's block. And I have to backtrack a little to see where I started, making it hard on myself, because that's when it stopped being fun. So then I erase the non-fun stuff and start again, this time having ***fun***. Throwing the baby and letting him/her save the day seemed fun to me! So this page shows me finding the right dialogue to end the book.

And that's that! Hope you liked the weirdest craziest book I ever made. Thanks for stopping by!

- Ryan